ZAC

OTHER TITLES AVAILABLE IN BUZZ BOOKS

FIREMAN SAM
1 Trevor's Trial Run
2 Norman's Spooky Night
3 A Bad Day For Dilys
4 Bella and The Bird's Nest
5 The Pride of Pontypandy
6 A Surprise for Sarah
7 Elvis's Experiment
8 Christmas in Pontypandy

TUGS
1 Kidnapped
2 Run Aground
3 Nothing to Declare
4 Treasure Hunt

BUGS BUNNY
1 Ali Baba Bunny
2 Knighty Knight Bugs
3 Broomstick Bunny
4 Mutiny on the Bunny

BARNEY
1 Barney and the Picnic
2 Barney's New Hair-Do
3 Barney Goes Shopping
4 Barney's Happy Christmas

MICRO MACHINES
1 Road Block
2 Hijack
3 Safe Breakers
4 Snowbound

GREMLINS
1 Don't Get Wet
2 Midnight Feast

First published 1991 by Buzz Books,
an imprint of the Octopus Publishing Group,
Michelin House, 81 Fulham Road, London SW3 6RB

LONDON · MELBOURNE · AUCKLAND

Toucan 'Tecs is developed from a series of
original books by Peter Lawson and Elizabeth Laird,
published by Heinemann Young Books
Character © 1988 Peter Lawson
Film © 1990 S4C/YTV
This edition © 1991 William Heinemann Ltd

ISBN 1 85591 127 2

Printed and bound in Great Britain by BPCC Hazell Books, Paulton and Aylesbury

IN

THE SNAIL'S TALE

Story by Elizabeth Laird
Characters devised by Peter Lawson
Illustrations by The County Studio

Zippi was bored. Zac was fed up.

Zippi tried telling a joke. Zac didn't laugh.

Zac tried pulling a funny face. Zippi didn't laugh.

Zac picked up a photo album.

"Oh look," he said. "Here we are with Samson on the first day he came."

"You were quite slim then, weren't you?"
said Zippi.

"You were quite good looking then,
weren't you?" said Zac.

They both sighed.

They began to daydream about their first
Toucan 'Tecs assignment . . .

"I'm bored," said Zac.

"I'm fed up," said Zippi. "What are we
going to do?"

"Let's go for a bike ride," said Zac.

"We haven't got any bikes," said Zippi.

"Let's play snakes and ladders," said Zac.

"There aren't any snakes here," said Zippi.

"Let's play houses," said Zac.

Zippi jumped up.

"*Play* houses?" he said. "No, we'll *make* a house! A proper one, with a door, and windows, and cupboards to keep nuts in!"

"Hooray!" shouted Zac. "No more messy old nests!"

9

They started building at once.

Zippi did the woodwork. He hit the nails on the head.

Zac did the plumbing. He put spanners in the works. They whistled as they worked.

They made so much noise that they didn't hear the Mad Ducks arrive.

10

The Mad Ducks were tired out.

"Ooh, my poor old wings," said one.

"I'm aching in every feather," said another.

"Hey!" said Red Leader. "Look over there! Someone's building a house for us! We'd better help them finish it off."

Zippi and Zac worked hard. Zippi's head
was in a cupboard.

"Pass the hammer, Zac," he called out.

A Mad Duck gave it to him.

"Thanks, Zac," said Zippi.

Zac was peering down a water pipe.

"Turn the water on, Zippi," he said.

A Mad Duck turned the water on.

"Thanks, Zippi," said Zac.

Soon the house was finished. Zippi and Zac stood back to admire it.

"Home sweet home," said Zippi.

Suddenly a head shot out of the door. And another. And another.

"Thanks for our nice new house!" the Mad Ducks said, slamming the door shut.

"Oi!" yelled Zippi. "What a nerve!"

"Hi!" shouted Zac. "Are you mad?"

The door opened again.

"What did you say?" said Red Leader.

"Are you mad?" said Zac.

"Yes," said Red Leader. "We're the Mad Ducks," and she slammed the door again.

"This is terrible," said Zippi.

"This is tragic," said Zac.

"This is terrific," said a voice.

"I've found some customers at last."

They turned round. A passing snail was hailing them.

"Samson, the travelling snailsman," he said. "At your service."

"Not today thank you," said Zippi.

"We don't want anything," said Zac.

"Surely you must want something," said Samson.

He popped inside his shell and then popped out again.

"A cuckoo clock?" he said. "Or a bicycle made for two?"

He popped in and out again.

"A palm tree in a pot? A set of china ducks?"

Zippi groaned.

"What's the matter?" said Samson. "You look shell-shocked."

"It's the ducks," said Zac. "They've nicked our house."

"Not – not the Mad Ducks, I hope?" said Samson.

Zippi and Zac nodded their heads.

Samson shook his.

"Only a great detective could solve this problem," he said. "Hey, wait a minute!"

He popped in and out again.

"Here we are," he said. "A Private Detective Kit! Special offer!"

"Zac," said Zippi. "I like it."

"Zippi," said Zac. "I love it."

"Samson," they said, "we'll buy it."

They bought it.

"And now," said Samson, "to get rid of those ducks. We need some paint, some brushes and a roll of canvas . . ."

A few hours later the job was done.

"Phew!" said Zippi.

"Wow!" said Zac.

"Right," said Samson. "Let's put the Mad Ducks in the picture."

He whistled. A duck stuck his head out of the window. "Hey!" he called to the others.

The Mad Ducks all stuck their heads out of the window.

"A fairy tale palace!" said one.

"A castle in the air!" said another.

"A home fit for ducks!" said Red Leader.

"It's much better than this place. What are we waiting for? Let's go."

"It's worked! We've done it!" shouted Zippi and Zac.

"Watch out! Mad Ducks overhead!" called Samson. "Let's get out of here."

"Quick march," said Zippi. "One, two, after you!"

"Three, four, knock at the door," said Zac, a few minutes later.

"Don't bother. Nobody's in," said
Samson. He slithered inside. "Oh my, what
a grand wee house."

"Of course," said Zac. "This is the house
that Zac built."

Zippi coughed.

"With a little help from your friend," he
said quietly.

Outside, mad quacking filled the air.

"If they go on like that," said Samson,
"they'll bring the house down."

Zippi looked out of the window.

"They have," he said.

The Mad Ducks all crawled out from
under the canvas.

"Who cares about castles anyway?" said
Red Leader. "Ducks need a home where the
dragonflies roam and the frogs and the
tadpoles play. Follow me!"

"Silly old houses," the ducks said, as they
spread out their wings and prepared for
take-off.

"Time for me to go too," said Samson sadly. "Someone, somewhere must want to buy a cuckoo clock and a potted palm and a bicycle made for two."

"Er, how about . . ." said Zippi.

"Um, what if . . ." said Zac.

"Yes?" said Samson.

"Do you like your job as a snailsman?" said Zippi.

"No," said Samson. "I hate it."

"Well then," said Zac, "why don't you stay here with us, and be our assistant? We're detectives now and detectives always have assistants."

"You mean it?" said Samson.

"We mean it," said Zippi.

"You've got yourselves a deal," said Samson.

Zippi started to snore and woke himself up.

"All that was a long time ago," he said. "How time flies!"

"How *do* you time flies?" said Zac. "You can't. They go too fast."

The door opened. Samson came in.

"Looking at old photos are you?" he said. "You *must* be bored."

"We are," said Zippi.

"Cheer up," said Samson. "A letter's just arrived. A new case, I expect."

"Where's it from?" said Zippi. "Iceland? Snowland? Greenland? Blueland?"

"Read it out, Samson," said Zippi. "I've got a funny feeling in my feathers. Another adventure's about to begin . . ."

ZIPPI